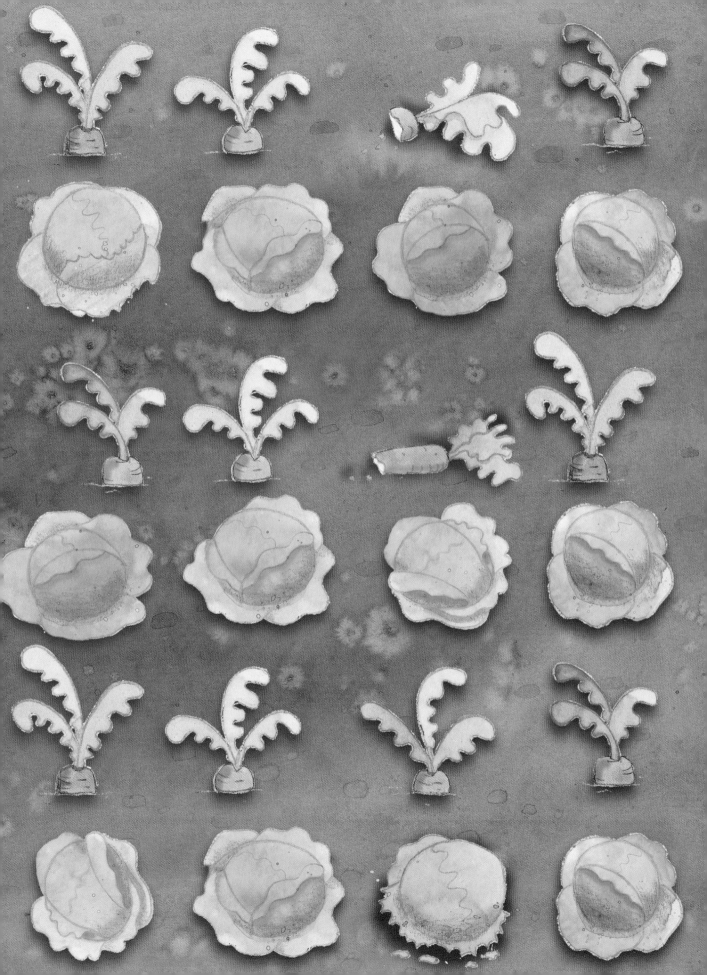

For Naomi in New York, and Emily who
still crosses days off the calendar! P.L.
For Daniel S.G.

First published in Great Britain in 2006
by Piccadilly Press Ltd,
5 Castle Road, London NWI 8PR
www.piccadillypress.co.uk

Text copyright © Paeony Lewis, 2006
Illustrations copyright © Sarah Gill, 2006

Designed by Simon Davis
Printed and bound by WKT in China
Colour reproduction by Dot Gradations

ISBN: 978 1 85340 814 4 (hardback)
978 1 85340 809 0 (paperback)

3 5 7 9 10 8 6 4 2

A catalogue record of this book is available from the British Library

Hurry Up, Birthday!

by **Paeony Lewis**
Illustrated by **Sarah Gill**

Piccadilly Press • London

Bouncer bounced out of bed.
He grabbed a crayon and crossed off another day.

"Hurry up, wake up!" he called to his sleepy brothers.
"Tomorrow's my birthday."

Muncher grunted.
Snoozer yawned.

At breakfast, Bouncer gobbled
carrots as fast as he could.
"Slow down,"
said Mother Rabbit.
"Can't," said Bouncer.
"I'm in a hurry."

"I'll eat your breakfast for you," offered Muncher.
"Thanks," Bouncer called as he hurried outside.

Every morning Bouncer practised bouncing.

Today he bounced twice as fast and twice as high.

Bouncer was in a hurry.

Bouncer bounced *faster* and *faster,*
and *higher* and *higher*.
"Do you want to play
hunt the berry?"
called Muncher.

"Sorry, can't stop," puffed Bouncer.
"I'm in a hurry."
Bouncer bounced so fast that he didn't
see the big branch above him.

"OUCH!"

"*Mum!*" shouted Muncher,
"*Bouncer's hurt himself.*"

"What happened?" asked Mother Rabbit.
"Bouncer bounced too fast," said Muncher.
"I'm in a hurry," said Bouncer, rubbing
his sore ear.

"I want today to go *really fast* because tomorrow's my birthday."

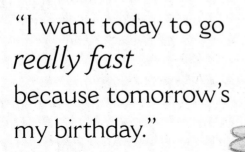

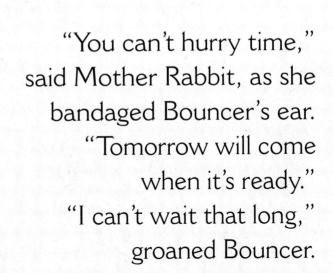

"You can't hurry time," said Mother Rabbit, as she bandaged Bouncer's ear. "Tomorrow will come when it's ready." "I can't wait that long," groaned Bouncer.

"Hurry up, birthday!"

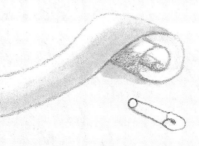

"Being busy might help you stop thinking about your birthday," said Mother Rabbit to Bouncer. "Why don't you find us a cabbage for lunch?"

"A *BIG* cabbage," said Muncher.

So off Bouncer bounced, down the hillside, past the sunflowers and across the meadow.

But when Bouncer reached the field of cabbages, all he could think about was how they looked like rows of birthday presents, all wrapped in green paper.

"Hurry up, birthday!" groaned Bouncer.

Bouncer handed Mother Rabbit a BIG cabbage.
"Now is it *nearly* my birthday?" he asked.
"Sorry, not yet," she said, shaking her head.
"What about cleaning the burrow? That'll stop you
thinking about your birthday. Your brothers could help."
Snoozer yawned. "I'm too tired."
"I'm too busy," said Muncher.
"I've got to find
a lost carrot."

"Hurry up, birthday!" groaned Bouncer.

Bouncer cleaned up anyway.

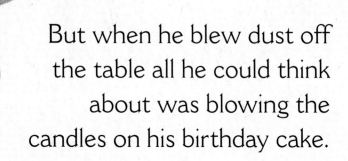

But when he blew dust off the table all he could think about was blowing the candles on his birthday cake.

"Hurry up, birthday," groaned Bouncer.

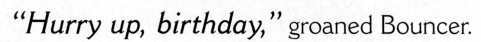

Finally, everything looked neat and sparkly.
"*Now* is it *nearly* my birthday?" Bouncer asked
Mother Rabbit.
"Soon," she said, tickling his good ear. "And while
you're waiting, do you have enough bounce
left for one last job?"

Mother Rabbit gave Bouncer a basket of apples
for Grandma Bake, and off he bounced.
Bouncer tried to think about Grandma's apple pies.

But he couldn't. All he could think about were
Grandma's wonderful apple *birthday cakes*.

Bouncer bounced faster. And faster. And . . . Oops!

Apples tumbled everywhere!

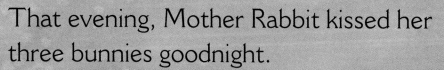

That evening, Mother Rabbit kissed her
three bunnies goodnight.
"The quicker you go to sleep, the quicker
tomorrow will come," she said to Bouncer.
"Waiting is *so* hard," said Bouncer.
"I wish *every* day was my birthday."

Mother Rabbit shook her head.
"Then birthdays wouldn't be special.
Now try to go to sleep."

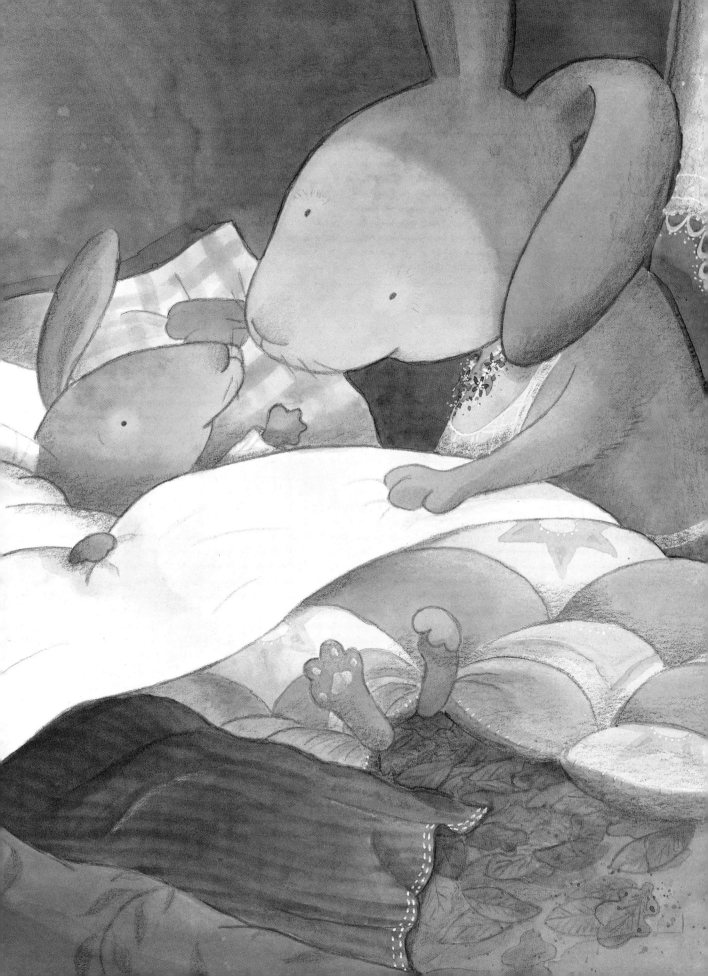

Snoozer and Muncher quickly fell asleep.
But Bouncer couldn't sleep. He watched the clock ticking.
"Hurry up, clock," whispered Bouncer.
But time moved slowly.

Bouncer gazed out of the burrow window.
"Hurry up, stars. Hurry up, moon," he whispered.
And the stars peeped out of the darkening
night and the moon moved slowly across the sky –
too slowly.

"Hurry up, birthday!"
yawned Bouncer, and he finally shut
his eyes. When he opened them
again it was . . .

. . . morning!

"HAPPY BIRTHDAY!"

Bouncer bounced a big,
slow birthday bounce.

Today Bouncer was going to do everything *slowly* because he didn't want to hurry his birthday.

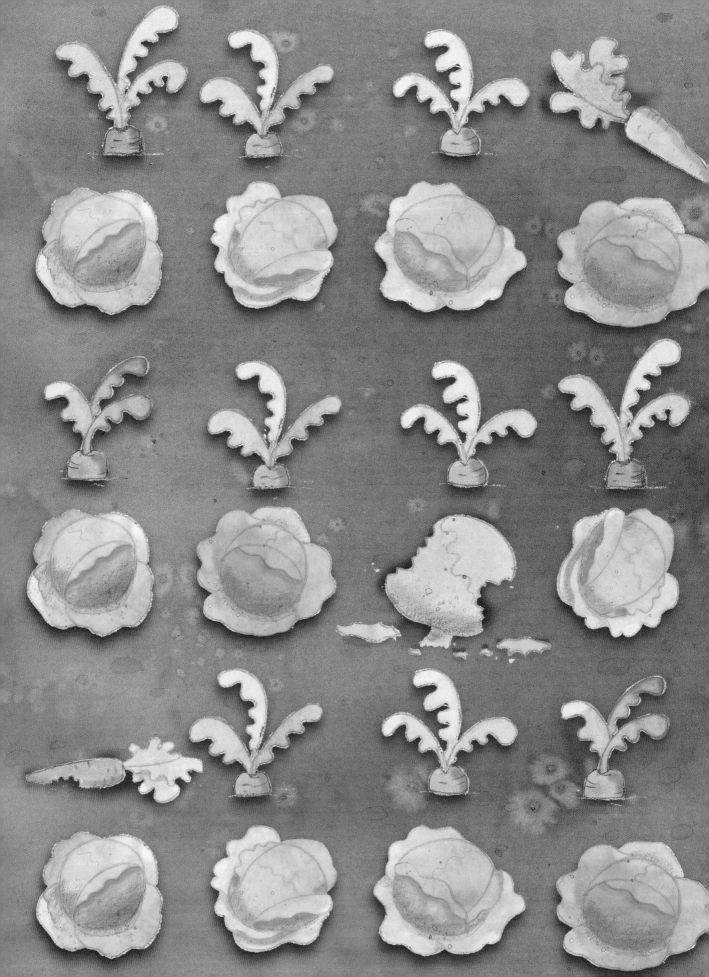